DATE DUE

DISCARD

PRINTED IN U.S.A.

For Sarah and Peter, the newest branch on the family tree.
— *M.H.*

Family is not about sharing a last name — it means always being there.
To my real close family. Para mis siete primos, con los que siempre cuento.
— *S.P.*

Published in 2016 by Eerdmans Books for Young Readers,
an imprint of Wm. B. Eerdmans Publishing Co.
2140 Oak Industrial Dr. NE
Grand Rapids, Michigan 49505
P.O. Box 163, Cambridge CB3 9PU U.K.

www.eerdmans.com/youngreaders

Manufactured at Tien Wah Press in Malaysia

16 17 18 19 20 21 22   8 7 6 5 4 3 2 1

ISBN 978-0-8028-5388-2

A catalog record of this book is available from the Library of Congress.

The illustrations were rendered digitally and with pen and ink.
The display type is set in Ad Lib Bt.
The text type was set in Humanist 777.

One Big Family

Written by
Marc Harshman

Illustrated by
Sara Palacios

EERDMANS BOOKS FOR YOUNG READERS

GRAND RAPIDS, MICHIGAN • CAMBRIDGE, U.K.

When the crickets sing
and the end of summer is near,
Grandma and Grandpa say
COME.

When the trip gets long
and no one is sleepy,
Dad says
COUNT.

When the car doors open
and Grandma and Grandpa
hold out their arms,
Mom says
KISS.

When the cooking is done
and we're gathered at the table,
Grandma says
EAT.

When the sun grows hot
and the water stays cold,
little brother says
SWIM.

When we go looking for honey
and the bees come chasing,
cousin Tommy says
RUN.

When the tents go up
and the campfire burns bright,
Uncle Jim says
SING.

When the campfire burns low
and Great-Grandpa tells stories,
everyone says
LISTEN.

When the lights are all out
and sister starts giggling,
someone says
SHUSH.

When it is time for breakfast
and the grown-ups are ready,
Aunt Jayne says
WASH.

When the boat hits the water
and the oars are locked in,
Uncle Bob says
ROW.

When we get downstream
and fishing poles are in our hands,
Grandpa says
WATCH.

And when we get back
and the piano is opened,
Leslie Ann says
PLAY.

When the littlest one tells her story
and bows when she's finished,
Aunt Jenny says
CLAP.

When we are all finally together,
one big family, standing tall in rows,
the photographer says
SMILE.

When it is weeks or months
or years later,
and we are all together again,
one big family,
we look at that picture,
and no one has to say
SMILE.

We just do.